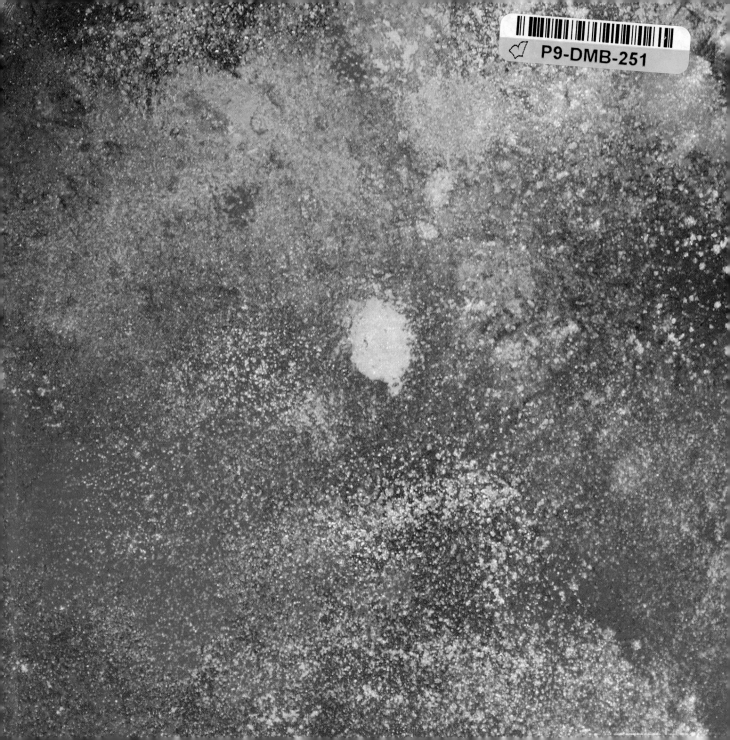

SABINE'S NOTEBOOK

In Which
The Extraordinary Correspondence of
Griffin & Sabine Continues

The best lack all conviction...

Written and Illustrated
by
Nick Bantock

Chronicle Books • San Francisco

Bantock, Nick.

Sabine's notebook : in which the extraordinary correspondence

of Griffin & Sabine continues / written and illustrated

by Nick Bantock.

p.   cm.

ISBN 0-8118-0180-2

1. Imaginary letters.   2. Toy and movable books–Specimens.

I. Title.

PR6052.A54S24 1992

823'.914–dc20

92-2638

CIP

Distributed in Canada by

Raincoast Books, 112 East Third Avenue,

Vancouver, B.C. V5T 1C8

10   9   8   7   6   5   4   3   2

Chronicle Books

275 Fifth Street

San Francisco, CA 94103

To Paul, Kate, Ruth, and Holly Kasasian

A HOODWINK

CONFIDENTIAL

FOR SABINE STROHEM
IN THE EVENT OF HER
ARRIVING AT —
41 YEATS AV.
LONDON
NW3

HAND

PERSONAL

Griffin – I am not surprised that you fled me. Your recent cards led me to expect an impulsive retreat. But I am saddened that I evoke fear in you.

I like your house and will be more than content to stay here. I have arranged to be away from the Sicmons until the end of July. As long as your quest takes no longer than that you can expect me to be here on your return.

Waiting all those years to find out who you were has prepared me for this; a little more waiting will do me no harm.

Sabine

Griffin – why is your studio stripped naked?

Griffin Moss
Gresham Hotel
O'Connell st
Dublin

I used some gold powder and an old air mail label I found in your kitchen. Do you mind?

SABINE/   FEB 4

I FEEL SO MUCH CALMER NOW THAT I'VE HEARD FROM
YOU. YOU SOUND SO GENTLE & TRANQUIL. HOW COULD
I HAVE IMAGINED THAT YOU WOULD BE THE DARK
CREATURE I AM SO TERRIFIED OF? WHEN I READ
YOUR CARD, I WANTED TO RETURN HOME IMMEDIATELY,
BUT I KNOW PRECISELY WHAT WOULD HAPPEN IF I DID.
I WOULD GO ALONG MERRILY UNTIL I CAME WITHIN
SIGHT OF MY DOOR, THEN I'D BEGIN TO SHAKE LIKE
A BONE IN A DOG'S MOUTH. BETTER I PUSH ON.
I CAME TO DUBLIN BECAUSE IT WAS MY GRANDFATHER'S
BIRTHPLACE & BECAUSE OF THE POWERFUL
WORDS THAT HAVE BEEN WRITTEN HERE.
AND FOR SOME REASON, THIS IS WHERE
MY JOURNEY BEGINS.
I WALKED IN THE WICKLOW MOUNTAINS

GRYPHON CARDS

YESTERDAY AND HEARD A SAD MUSIC.
THE SLOPES WERE SO SOFT & GREEN
THAT I BEGAN TO CRAVE COLD MARBLE —
TOMORROW I FLY TO FLORENCE.
I DON'T KNOW WHERE I'LL BE STAYING, PLEASE
WRITE TO ME C/O POSTE RESTANTE.
ALL MY LOVE   GRIFFIN
ANYTHING IN THE HOUSE IS YOURS
TO USE.

SABINE STROHEM
41 YEATS AV.
LONDON NW3
ENGLAND

EIRE

AER-PHOST
AIR MAIL

Griffin Moss
Poste Restante
Florence
Italy

Griffin – I am still in the first flush of excitement at being here. I wish I had you to show me around, but I follow my nose and have seen many amazing things.

I think I was prepared for everything except the people. There are so many of them. I tried traveling on the underground train when they were all going to work – it was extraordinary, bodies pressed together like fish crushed in a net. After one stop I had to go above ground to feel the sky again. I saw you painting last night, a woman in mist. It brought you close to me.

                          Sabine

Who does the grey cat belong to? Should I feed it?

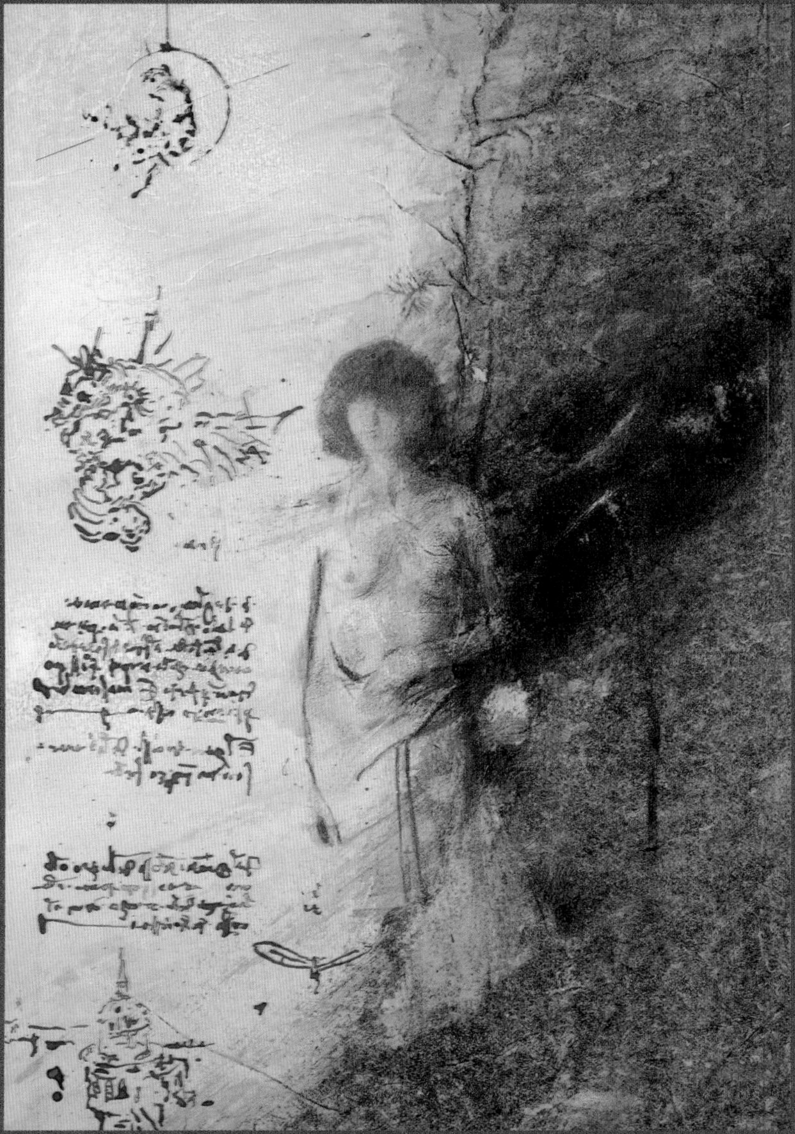

SABINE / FEB 11
YOU SPEAK OF LONDON
BEING FULL OF PEOPLE.
WELL FLORENCE HAS ITS
SHARE TOO, MOSTLY PACKS OF
TOURISTS DETERMINED TO GET
THEIR MONEY'S WORTH BY TEARING THROUGH EVERY
MUSEUM IN THE CITY. BUT THEY DON'T MATTER
BECAUSE EVERYTHING ELSE IS SOOTHING TO ME.
THE ARCHITECTURE, THE SCULPTURE, THE LAND ITSELF
ARE ALL SO MAGNIFICENT THAT I'M HEALED.
I MUST BE — WHY ELSE SHOULD I BE SO HAPPY?
THIS JOURNEY HAS TAKEN ON THE CHARACTER OF
A PILGRIMAGE: GRIFFIN MOSS PAYS HOMAGE AT
THE ALTAR OF HIS MASTERS.
I'M GOING TO STAY A FEW DAYS LONGER & GIVE
MYSELF A CHANCE TO SEE THE CHURCHES.
I HAD A WONDERFUL SENSUOUS DREAM LAST
NIGHT. I WAS AT THE PALAZZO DI MEDICI
TALKING TO LORENZO HIMSELF, WHEN YOU
EMERGED FROM A SMOKEY WALL & ENVELOPED
ME.
I MISS YOU   GRIFFIN

SABINE STROHEM
41 YEATS AV.
LONDON NW3
ENGLAND

HAVING NO MORE PRINTED CARDS WITH ME. I'M MAKING ONE-OFFS LIKE YOU.

PER VIA AEREA
PAR AVION
Mod. 24-R

20 LIRE
POSTE ITALIANE

150 LIRE
POSTE ITALIANE

PAGE FROM LEONARDO'S MISSING SKETCHBOOK

Griffin—You gave me an idea—
instead of wandering haphazardly
around, I decided to take a tour
of London's churches. The big
ones, like St. Paul's, I found grand but empty.
Then I came upon one that was different.
It was a dark place, steeped in death. As
I stood looking at it, I felt its roots running
below the city like a black twin to the underground.
Enough playing the tourist. It is time I get down to
some work. Italy suits you, my love. But be a little
cautious; the eye of the storm is a deceptive place.
— Sabine
The stamp on the front is a printers' proof. The last I
drew up before I left Katie — camels make me laugh.

Griffin Moss
Poste Restante
Florence
Italy

SABINE/   FEB 26
YOU WERE RIGHT— AGAIN. AS SOON AS I LEFT
ITALY, MY CONFIDENCE DRAINED AWAY.
GREECE IS A PLEASANT ENOUGH COUNTRY, BUT
I'M A TOTAL STRANGER. I IMAGINED BEING HEROIC
AGAINST A PERFECT BLUE AND WHITE ISLAND
BACKGROUND. FAT CHANCE. INSTEAD, BLACK CLOUDS ARE CIRCLING
AROUND ME AND I'M GETTING SCARED AGAIN. YOUR CARD DIDN'T
HELP EITHER; YOUR DESCRIPTION OF THE DARK CHURCH RANG ALL
KINDS OF UNPLEASANT BELLS.
I NEED TO HOLD YOUR HAND. I'M GETTING NUMB.
IS THIS THE NIGHT BEFORE I CROSS INTO NO-MAN'S LAND?

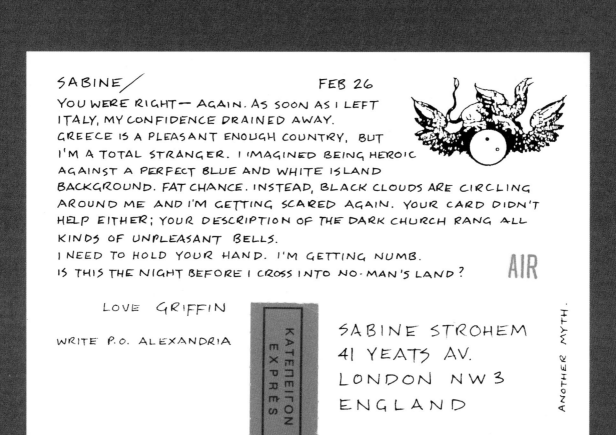

AIR

        LOVE GRIFFIN

    WRITE P.O. ALEXANDRIA

ΚΑΤΕΠΕΙΓΟΝ
ΕΧΡRΕS

SABINE STROHEM
41 YEATS AV.
LONDON NW3
ENGLAND

ANOTHER MYTH.

crystalline
limestone

Griffin — Your preparations for "crossing into no-man's land" have the sound of a death wish. Why not try to view the next stage of your journey as a transition? Choose reassuring thoughts. Remember, I'm holding the string end, and I won't allow you to disappear into oblivion.

I've set up camp in the British Museum, drawing by day and then returning to paint in your studio at night. The museum is cosy. The dust and the narrow shafts of sunlight remind me of my father's study.

Keep strong   Sabine

You still haven't told me why your studio's empty.

— the Sumerian bear on the front is meant to be a hostility symbol. But it looks melancholy to me.

By air mail
Par avion

Griffin Moss
Poste Restante
Alexandria
Egypt

hands/feet

He cannot pull free so he continues to push

SABINE STROHEM
41 YEATS AV.
LONDON NW3
ENGLAND

GRIFFIN MOSS
℅ POSTE RESTANTE
ALEXANDRIA

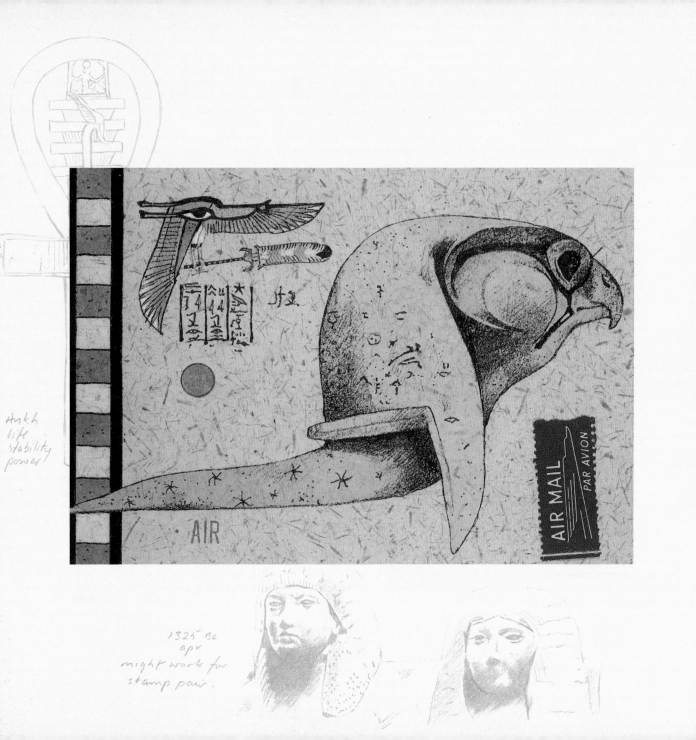

Ankh
life
stability
power

AIR

AIR MAIL
PAR AVION

1325 Bc
apx
might work for
stamp pair.

Griffin – You must be blessed. In Sicmon mythology, wandering warriors place themselves at the service of worthy travelers. They are reputed to keep Death from becoming greedy.

The figure in your painting appears especially formidable — with him around, I know that you will be able to confront almost any threat.

I've been drawing in the museum's Egyptian gallery. The silent stones fill me with awe — they are sublimely sophisticated. The city's neon lights seem naive in comparison, like childrens' toys.

　　　　　Take heart Sabine.

Minaloushe came into the house today — you see I too have been honoured.

SABINE/ APRIL 5
I WAS CLINGING TO LOGIC LIKE A LIFE BUOY.
NOW, IN THE FLICK OF AN EYE I'M TRYING TO
FOLLOW INTUITION. I SEE A REFLECTION OF A
SAMURAI IN THE GLASS OF A PAINTING AND I
COME TO JAPAN — REASON IS DISCARDED
& I'M JUST GOING WHERE THE VOICES OF THE MOMENT SEEM TO SEND
ME. I'M THE BARBARIAN STALKING THE TEMPLES OF KYOTO FOR LONG-
DEPARTED WISDOM; I WALLOW IN THE AESTHETICS HOPING THAT THEY
WILL PURIFY THE BEHOLDER.
THESE ARE MY INTROSPECTIVE WHIMPERINGS. I'M A SELF-INDULGENT
CHILD — WHY CAN'T I GROW UP? I ASK THAT SINCERELY. IF YOU KNOW,
TELL ME.
IF I COULD DRAW THE WAY I FEEL ABOUT YOU, I WOULD.

LOVE GRIFFIN

c/o P.O. KYOTO

PAR AVION
航 空

SABINE STROHEM
41 YEATS AV.
LONDON NW 3
ENGLAND

Head of the chariot horse of Selene (the Moon)

Nambokucho

Griffin
It seems to me that you are in the process of growing up right now. That, amongst other reasons, is why I'm waiting for you. As for self-indulgence I think not. This trip is something you must do.

I've discovered an ice cream parlour opposite the Roundhouse that serves perfect coffee. I'm plagued by the constant temptation to ride the 19 bus to Chalk Farm and drink a cup. Could be sexual frustration (my father had me read Freud). Maybe if you were here I wouldn't want. Then again we children might go together.
                    Sabine

Griffin Moss
Poste Restante
Kyoto
Japan

AIR

SABINE/   MAY 2
I WISHED TO BE SOMEWHERE TRULY OLD, AND THUS, BY
VARIOUS CONVOLUTED ROUTES, I FOUND MYSELF HERE,
AMONG THESE BUSHMEN. THEY ARE FASCINATING PEOPLE.
THEY NAVIGATE THEIR LAND BY SONGS AND STORIES.
AN ELDER WHO HAS BEEN KIND TOOK ME TO MEET HIS
MOTHER. SHE GRASPED MY HAND, STARED AT ME
LONG AND HARD, AND THEN TOLD ME THAT "MY" BACK
WAS OPEN." SHE SHUFFLED INTO HER HUT & EMERGED
WITH A FEATHER AND THEN SHE BEGAN TO STROKE MY
BACK WITH IT. AFTERWARDS, I OFFERED TO PAY HER,
BUT SHE MADE SPUTTERING NOISES, SO I GAVE HER
A PICTURE I'D DONE OF A TWISTED TREE.
THIS PRODUCED A HUGE SMILE, AND I WAS MUCH
CONGRATULATED BY THOSE GATHERED AROUND.
                          LOVE GRIFFIN

CAN YOU STILL SEE ME?
WILL PASS THROUGH BRISBANE – WRITE THERE.

AIR MAIL

PAR AVION

RUNNING TO & FRO THE MOON

SABINE STROHEM
41 YEATS AV.
LONDON NW3
ENGLAND

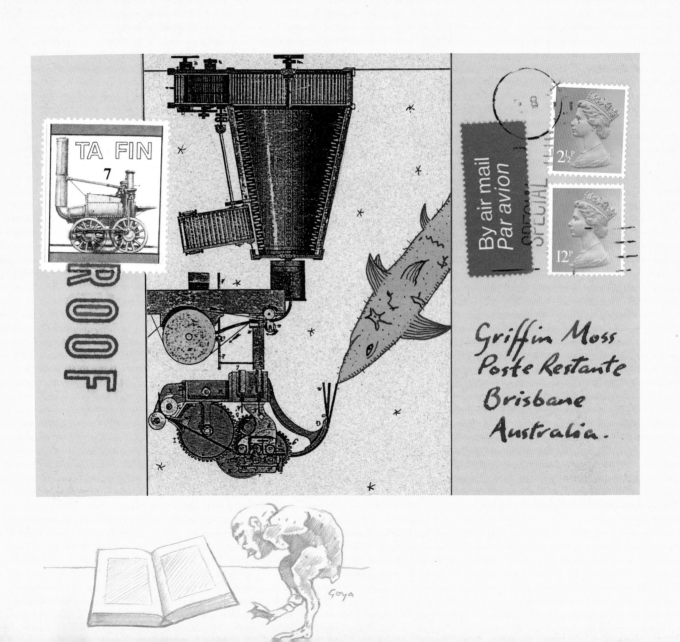

TA FIN

7

PROOF

By air mail
Par avion

SPECIAL

2½P

12P

Griffin Moss
Poste Restante
Brisbane
Australia.

Goya

found Griffin symbols in Flood the Hermetic

PROOF TA FIN 7 7

I decided this design was a little too self indulgent.

SABINE/   MAY 29
YOU SHAME ME. YOU HAVE MUCH MORE FAITH IN
ME THAN I DO. THE OPENNESS OF YOUR LOVE
OVERWHELMS ME.
OF COURSE I LOVE YOU. AS FOR LIKING MYSELF —
POSSIBLY I CAN ACHIEVE THAT WHEN I'M LESS PRONE
TO BOUTS OF SELF-PITY. PART OF ME DESPERATELY
WANTS TO GO TO YOU RIGHT NOW. BUT I'M COMMITTED
TO FINISHING THAT WHICH I HAVE STARTED. IF I AM
TO FIND MY COURAGE AND UNDERSTAND THE
CONNECTION BETWEEN US, THEN MY OUTWARD
VOYAGE ENDS IN THE SICMONS.
WITH ALL MY SOUL GRIFFIN.
I HAD A REVELATION — IN A MOMENT'S DAYDREAM
I GLIMPSED A PAINTING OF A MASK. I'M CERTAIN
IT WAS YOURS.

Australia 45¢

10¢ AUSTRALIA

star sapphire

AIR MAIL
PAR AVION

SABINE STROHEM
4 YEATS AV.
LONDON NW3
ENGLAND

29
21

WRITE ℅ THE MENDANA HOTEL HONIARA

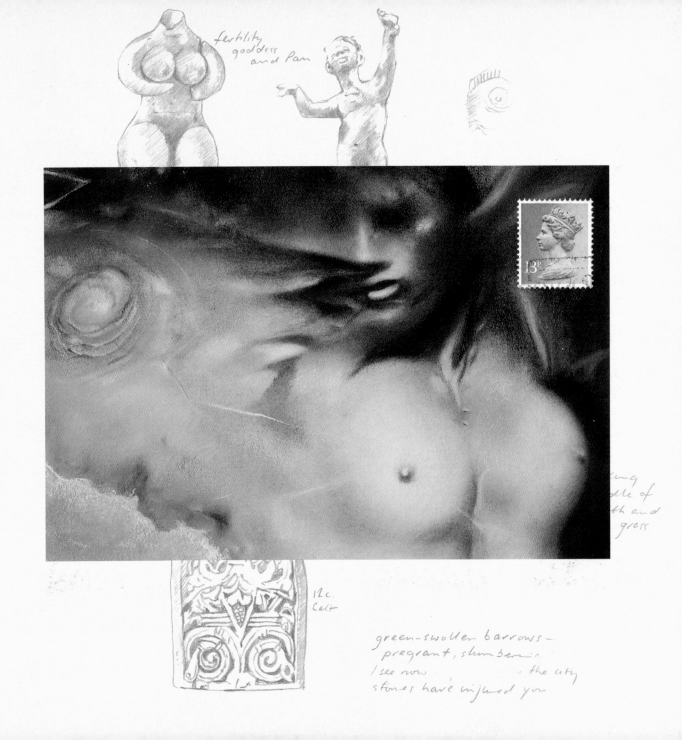

fertility
goddess
and Pan

13ᵖ

ing
dle of
th and
gress.

12c.
Celt

green-swollen barrows—
pregnant, slumbering
I see now . . . . the city
stones have injured you

Griffin — I had thought to stay in the city in case you returned suddenly. That seems unlikely now, so I've come out to the countryside near Dorset.

I have been in sad danger of confusing London and England. Two very different places!

I'm sitting on top of the rolling earthmound known as Maiden's Castle. It is a handmade hill that purrs quietly like an old slumbering creature. I feel rejuvenated — I hadn't realized what a prisoner I'd become. The area you enter is dangerous. Beware such things as abrupt changes of weather and never underestimate the sea.

Sabine

griffin — part of armlet 4ᵗᶜ BC

PAR AVION

Griffin Moss
Mendana Hotel
Honiara
Guadalcanal

Remind him of the sea's danger.

AIR MAIL

CHECKED

SABINE STROHEM
41 YEATS AV.
LONDON NW3
ENGLAND

35 CENTS BRITISH SOLOMON ISLANDS
Dendrobium cuthbertsonii

replace moth
body with
human

a time
was a lonely
wolf lonelier
than the angels.

Griffin —
You have survived.
Are you coming home when your strength returns?
Will I see you at last?
I alternate between storms of impatience and lulls of peace.
I draw in Highgate Cemetery, communing with my sisters. I can work there without constant intrusions from people looking over my shoulder. The museum was becoming impossible. I am trying to concentrate on a series of stone angels for Sicmon's Christmas stamps.
Though, really, I'm waiting for you
— love Sabine

Griffin Moss
9 Hospital
Honiara, Guadalcanal
Solomon Islands

I think you cannot know.

SABINE   JULY 20

MY MIND HAS BEEN CLEARING STEADILY.
I KNOW WHO YOU ARE, WHAT WE ARE, AND
WHAT WE WILL BE TO ONE ANOTHER.
I WILL BE HOME ON THE 23 RD. PROBABLY
THE SAME DAY THAT THIS CARD IS DELIVERED.

                          GRIFFIN

PAR AVION

FRANCE 1,00   FRANCE 1,20

SABINE STROHEM
41 YEATS AV.
LONDON NW3
ENGLAND

Griffin Moss returned, as promised, on the 23rd of July.

His house was empty and showed no signs of
anyone having been there.   But

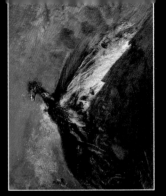

Hardly are
   those words
      out when...

Griffin

I received your Paris card.

I waited, but you did not return on the 23rd.

I waited until the 31st, but you did not
return.

What happened?

Where are you?

Write to me, Griffin.

Sabine

Special

Griffin Moss
41 Yeats Av
London NW3
England.